"The story is beautifully written, funny and interesting. My favourite part was learning that Thunder (the cat) could talk!"
Joe, age 9

I wish I was part of the Playdate Adventure Club. It's exciting that the characters go on adventures together, change things from wrong to right and help the environment."
Lucy, age 8

"Better than brilliant."
Alexander J, age 9

"This book taught me all about the dangers of light pollution for nocturnal animals. I won't sleep with the light on anymore."
Zadie, age 6

Meet the
Playdate Adventurers!

Katy

Chatty, sociable and kind. She's the glue that holds the Playdate Adventure Club together. Likes animals (especially cats) and has big dreams of saving the world one day.

Cassie

Shy but brave when she needs to be. She relies on her friends to give her confidence. Loves dancing, especially street dance, but only in the privacy of her bedroom.

Zia

Loud, confident and intrepid. She's a born leader but can sometimes get carried away. Likes schoolwork and wants to be a scientist when she's older, just like her mum.

Luca

The newest member of the club. He's shy, like his cousin Cassie, but not when it comes to going on an adventure. Is completely obsessed with watching nature programmes.

Thunder

Big, white and fluffy with grey ears, paws and tail. He's blind in one eye, but that's what makes him extra special. Likes chasing mice and climbing trees, but hates water. Is also a cat.

**Join the friends on
all their Playdate Adventures**

THE MIDNIGHT MOON

FEAST

Emma Beswetherick
Illustrated by Anna Woodbine

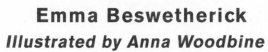

ROCK THE BOAT

A Rock the Boat Book

First published by Rock the Boat,
an imprint of Oneworld Publications, 2022

Text copyright © Emma Beswetherick, 2022
Illustration copyright © The Woodbine Workshop, 2022

The moral right of Emma Beswetherick and the Woodbine Workshop
to be identified as the Author and Illustrator of this work respectively has
been asserted by them in accordance with the Copyright, Designs, and
Patents Act 1988

ISBN 978-0-86154-338-0 (paperback)
ISBN 978-0-86154-339-7 (ebook)

Printed and bound in Great Britain by Clays Ltd, Elcograf S.p.A.

This book is a work of fiction. Names, characters, businesses, organisations,
places and events are either the product of the author's imagination or are used
fictitiously. Any resemblance to actual persons, living or dead, events
or locales is entirely coincidental.

Oneworld Publications
10 Bloomsbury Street, London, WC1B 3SR, England

Stay up to date with the latest books,
special offers, and exclusive content from
Rock the Boat with our newsletter

Sign up on our website
rocktheboatbooks.com

For my children, Archie and Isla, and their friends,
for the fun and laughter they bring to any sleepover –
and the secret treats they hide under their pillows!

CHAPTER ONE

The clock chimed six times in the hall and Cassandra's heart skipped a beat. She'd ploughed on through five days of school, three pieces of homework, a maths *and* an English test, two dance lessons and her aunt's surprise birthday celebration. Her cousin Luca had stayed on after the party and now they were both lying on the sofa, waiting for their two best friends to arrive – *any minute now.*

"So, what do you think we should do this evening?" Cassandra asked, jumping up and spinning around in one of her favourite street dance moves. "Apart from eating an enormous midnight feast!"

Luca was staring at the TV screen, too engrossed in a nature documentary to answer.

"Earth calling Luca," she said, waving her hands in front of his face. But her cousin didn't get a chance to respond. The doorbell rang and she sprinted across the lounge and out into the hall.

"Slow down, Cassie," her mum called as Cassandra raced towards the front door, with Luca hot on her heels. "Your friends will still be there, even if you walk, you know."

But Cassandra was already hurling the door open, throwing her arms around Katy and Zia and flinging their bags, pillows and sleeping bags down on the floor.

"Hi, girls, it's good to see you!" Cassandra's

mum laughed, helping to hang coats and place shoes tidily in the shoe rack. "Maybe Cassie will finally be able to sit still now that you're here."

Katy's dad smiled from the doorway. "Girls, be good, OK?" he called. "I'll pick you both up after breakfast tomorrow." Then, turning to Cassandra's mum: "Just call if there's a problem and I'll be straight round."

"Don't worry," said Cassandra's mum in her soft Jamaican accent. "They've been asking for a sleepover for weeks. I've even agreed to let them eat pizza in Cassie's bedroom. I'm sure I won't be seeing much of them this evening."

Even as she said it, the four friends were disappearing up the stairs.

As Cassandra closed her bedroom door, Katy and Zia began unpacking their overnight bags.

"I haven't been on a sleepover for ages," Zia announced, pulling out an endless supply of books and stationery and cuddly toys from her backpack. "I didn't really know what to pack."

"Me neither," giggled Katy. "Although there's one thing I knew I *had* to bring." As if on cue, a pair of grey ears poked from the top of her overnight bag, followed by a whiskery grey face, the tip of a grey tail and, finally, a large, fluffy white body.

"THUNDER!" everyone squealed, as Katy's ragdoll cat leapt from her bag and began parading around the bedroom, winking with his one working eye.

"Now all the gang are here we can have a proper adventure!" Cassandra exclaimed.

"He's promised not to be grumpy today, haven't you, Thunder?" Katy said, rubbing her cat along his back, just the way he liked it. His tail shot straight in the air.

Thunder was the fifth – and most special – member of their Playdate Adventure Club. Every time they had a playdate, some incredible form of magic turned their imaginary adventure into a *real-life* amazing one. The club was top secret and the coolest thing Cassandra had ever been a part of.

While her friends continued fussing over Thunder, Cassandra began rummaging in her bedside cabinet.

"Sweets for the midnight feast!" She beamed as she pulled a large tin from the cupboard and popped open its lid.

"How m-many sweets do you have in there, C-Cassie?" Luca gasped, his dark eyes wide and round.

"*Too* many, probably." Cassandra giggled. "But isn't that the point?"

"You can never have too many sweets," said Katy, grabbing a packet of cola bottles from her bag and emptying them into the tin. "Especially fizzy ones."

"I like the ones you suck until they're *so* tiny you can't even tell if they're in your mouth anymore." Zia fumbled around in her backpack until she found a packet of gobstoppers to add to the collection.

"The s-sourer the better for me," said Luca. "I love the ones that m-make you screw your face up. Like this!" he exclaimed, pulling a silly expression.

Everyone laughed.

"Hey, remember the last time we tried to have a midnight feast?" asked Zia, staring wistfully at Katy and Cassandra. Then she turned to Luca, who hadn't been there. "We fell asleep too early and ended up missing midnight," she explained.

"At breakfast, none of us wanted sweets anymore," added Cassandra.

"We c-can't let that happen tonight," said Luca.

"Agreed," said Katy. "We need to keep ourselves busy. Luca, did you bring your new telescope? I've been dying to see it."

Luca nodded. "And I've already st-started setting it up. Look, by the w-window." He walked over to Cassandra's desk and began pulling more bits of apparatus out of a box.

Luca had a stammer and often felt embarrassed about speaking, especially in class. Luckily, he felt comfortable around his cousin and friends, and now they hardly noticed when he stumbled over a word.

"So how does it work?" asked Katy, going over to join him. "Can you really see all the planets and stars in the sky?"

"Not all of them." Luca shook his head, fixing the long tube onto a tripod base. "You'd need a really p-powerful telescope to see some of the f-far away planets and stars. B-but on a clear night, you can see Mars, Jupiter and Saturn through this one."

 "Can we look for them now?" asked Katy.

Luca shook his head while fixing the final piece of the telescope into place. "You w-won't be able to see anything yet. It's still too light outside. We'll have to w-wait until it gets p-properly dark."

"Then let's get ready for the sleepover,"

Cassandra suggested, dragging three inflatable mattresses from under her bed. "Look, Mum's blown up our camping mats. There's one for each of you."

"Bagsy I sleep next to your bed," Zia said hurriedly.

Katy shrugged, not really minding. "Thunder and I are happy by the wardrobe."

"Then I'll go by the w-window," said Luca. "So I'm closest to my telescope."

One by one, they disappeared into the bathroom to change into pyjamas. Yet there really wasn't any chance of them falling asleep before midnight. They were way too excited about pizza in bed. Not to mention their midnight feast. And they still hadn't discussed where they were going on their next magical adventure.

CHAPTER TWO

Cassandra's bedroom was a cacophony of chatter and laughter. Her mum had delivered two large boxes of pizza and they'd all eaten hungrily, careful not to let any delicious stringy cheese slide off the top and onto the carpet. Their conversation moved swiftly from teachers and school lunches, to favourite pop songs, to whether any child in the world *really* liked the taste of liquorice. *Ugh!* The best topic, however, they were saving until last.

"So where should we go on our next adventure?" asked Zia, tossing her last bit of pizza crust into the box.

They looked at each other eagerly.

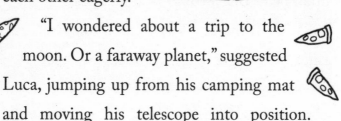

"I wondered about a trip to the moon. Or a faraway planet," suggested Luca, jumping up from his camping mat and moving his telescope into position. "Actually, can you t-turn the lights off, Cassie? I think it's finally d-dark enough outside."

Cassandra flicked the light switch above her bed. At once, the room was plummeted into darkness.

"P-perfect. Now, who wants to go first?" Luca put his eye to the eyepiece and gazed out into the wide night sky. "I'll just f-focus the lens and then... Hey, that's weird. The stars look really p-pale tonight." He twisted the dial one way,

14

then the other, before giving up and staring back at his friends. "I think we have a p-problem," he sighed. "There's still t-too much light."

"Too much light?" Cassandra asked, sitting up in bed. "But my room's in darkness!"

"Yes, but there's a f-full moon tonight," said Luca, pointing through the window.

Zia and Katy walked over to join him.

"That moon's enormous!" Zia gasped. "It's lighting up the whole sky!"

"The streetlights and headlights are a problem too," muttered Katy, frowning. "And so many houses still have lights on."

"Why does that matter?" Zia looked confused.

"Because of light pollution," Katy explained.

Everyone was up now, peering through the window at the hazy glow lighting up the dark street outside.

"Is light pollution bad?" asked Cassandra, amazed she hadn't noticed it before.

"It's not *good*," answered Katy. "Especially for nocturnal animals. They can see and hunt much better in the dark. It's why floodlights at sports stadiums are controversial."

"What's *c-controversial*?" asked Luca.

"Basically, it means that some people like the idea, and some people don't," Zia chipped in. "What if you can't sleep in the dark, though? Surely a few lights at night aren't bad for the animals?"

Katy went to answer, but Cassandra got in first. "Zia…you don't sleep with the light *on*, do you?"

A blush crept across Zia's cheeks. "Only a night light. I get a bit scared sometimes. That's all."

"But you're the bravest of all of us," Katy added, surprised by this discovery.

16

"We should help you," Cassandra announced, turning the light back on and laying a hand gently on Zia's shoulder. "How about a night-time adventure?"

"Hey, that's not a bad idea," Katy said. "You're scared of the dark, so what better way to face your fears?"

Zia looked uncomfortable – the blush had drained from her cheeks. "I'm just not sure," she mumbled.

But a plan was forming in Cassandra's head. She grabbed Zia's hands and looked her squarely in the eyes. "Listen, you always tell us we need to face *our* fears. You've been there for us on every adventure – now it's our turn to be there for you!"

"Cassie's right, Zia." Luca smiled warmly. "Remember my f-first adventure, when a flying safari jeep appeared in Katy's b-bedroom.

17

There's no way I was going to get on it at first. I was t-terrified! But you said you'd be there for me, and I b-believed you."

"We could have the midnight feast on our night-time adventure!" Katy blurted excitedly.

Cassandra squealed, then clapped her hands together. "Imagine eating all those treats under a full moon."

"In a m-magical clearing, with m-magical creatures," added Luca.

"And magical food," Katy added. "It really would be the best midnight feast of all time!"

Zia's cheeks had returned to their normal colour now and she gazed hopefully at her friends. "Do you really think I can do it?"

"We know you can!" they all chimed, and they came together in a big group hug.

At that moment, Thunder leapt onto Cassandra's desk, meowing loudly and nudging the telescope with his head.

"What is it, Thunder?" asked Katy. "Are you excited by a moonlit midnight feast adventure too?"

But Thunder carried on meowing and rubbing himself against the eyepiece.

Suddenly, Katy pulled Thunder into her arms. "Thunder, you're a g-genius," she cried, kissing the top of his head, which he batted away with his paw. "The telescope," she said to the others. "I think Thunder's saying we could use it – to transport us somewhere. Like the jeep when we went on safari. Or the rocket that took us to the stars."

"Maybe it could become a kind of portal?" Cassandra asked.

Thunder meowed.

"I think that's exactly what Thunder was trying to say," Katy laughed.

"Great p-plan!" Luca exclaimed, excited that his telescope might come in useful after all. "What do you think, Zia?"

Everyone looked at her, keeping fingers and toes crossed that she trusted her friends enough to get on board with the plan.

"Well, as long as it doesn't take us *too* far from home… I think it's definitely the best way to stay awake until midnight." Zia grinned.

Everyone laughed and nodded in agreement.

"Right, first we need to pack our midnight feast provisions," said Cassandra, grabbing a backpack from behind her and pushing the tin of treats deep down inside. Before she zipped the bag closed, she also grabbed a bag of cat treats for Thunder and stuffed that in too.

Then she gathered everyone in a circle, Thunder in the

20

middle, and looked at the four expectant faces staring back at her. It was a big responsibility hosting a playdate adventure. She had to plan things quickly – she didn't want to let them down. "OK, now we should all close our eyes and imagine Luca's telescope getting bigger. Imagine it transforming into an enormous portal we can walk through, one that can shoot us straight into a magical world. Imagine a forest full of night-time creatures, the brightest, fullest milky-white moon and an inky sky filled to bursting with stars."

Cassandra dared a quick peek at her friends, who were diligently imagining the adventure she'd described, eyes shut tight. Thunder was curled on the floor, also with his eye closed. Cassandra squeezed her lids together one more time and said the words her friends were all longing to hear:

"Everyone, repeat after me: I wish to go on an adventure."

CHAPTER THREE

"*I wish to go on an adventure,*" everyone chanted.

Immediately, their bodies started pulsing with a familiar feeling of electricity, firing hot, then cold, fizzing then cracking, until their hairs were standing on end from the tops of their heads to the tips of their toes. The floor was also shaking – buzzing and vibrating so much it felt like the room was moving beneath their feet.

Only when the sensations had stopped did they dare open their eyes.

"OH!" cried Cassandra.

"MY!" squealed Katy.

"GOODNESS!" shouted Zia.

The object that now stood before them made their chins drop one by one to the floor.

"Is that really m-my telescope?" screamed Luca, as they stared at the enormous, whizzy contraption now at least twenty times the size it was before.

The eyepiece was bigger than Thunder, the lens at the other end at least the size of Cassandra's bedroom door. It was now on the floor, tilted up towards the window like a great tunnel towards the sky. The black plastic casing was flashing a multitude of neon lights, like the disco lights at the roller disco Zia liked to go to.

"Who wants to go first?" asked Cassandra, smiling uncertainly at her friends.

"You know, for the first time ever, I don't think I'm going to volunteer," Zia answered, tugging nervously at the hem of her pyjamas. "Hey, have you seen our new outfits?"

They all looked down and marvelled at their new fluffy boot slippers and warm, fleecy dressing gowns, decorated with moons and stars. Even Thunder had a fleecy moon-and-stars scarf tied snuggly around his neck, which he was pulling at with a put-out look on his face.

Cassandra and Katy held on to Zia's hands and squeezed, as Luca stepped forwards towards the telescope.

"I'm happy to go first," he said. "It's my t-telescope, so I feel kind of r-responsible."

Cassandra breathed a sigh of relief.

"Thanks, Luca," she said, swallowing hard. "Maybe you should crouch down, then look through the eyepiece and…"

But Luca had already knelt on the floor and now his body was spinning fast like a whirlwind. The twirling blur got smaller and smaller, until finally he was sucked through the eyepiece and disappeared in a blinding flash of light. *POOF!*

Everyone stood there, stunned into silence. Only Thunder seemed unfazed by what had happened.

"Er – do you think he's OK?" asked Zia.

"I really hope so," Katy gasped. "I'm not sure I even thought about that part of the adventure. Is that how you both imagined it?"

Cassandra and Zia shook their heads. Then all three turned to look at Thunder, who sat casually washing one ear.

"OK, well, we'd better go and find him." Cassandra hoisted her backpack onto her back and took a few hesitant steps towards the telescope. "I'll see you on the other side." She crouched down by the eyepiece and immediately began to spin. Faster and faster. Faster and faster. She couldn't see. She couldn't hear. Everything was fuzzy. She felt the insides of her body squeezed tighter and tighter. Then, as quickly as the spinning had started, it stopped. She shot into the air like a cork from a bottle and landed with a *THUD* on cold, hard ground.

THUD – another body landed next to her. Then another, and another. The five adventurers sat in the darkness, winded, wiggling their fingers, toes and paws to check they were still in one piece.

Luca got up first and helped Cassandra to her feet. She wobbled, legs still shaky from the portal. "Is everyone OK?" she said.

"Not really," Zia whispered.

"We're right with you, Zia," Katy said, grabbing her friend's hand and pulling her up to standing. "And I'm also a bit scared – I promise you're not alone."

"Well, I *love* the dark," said another male voice.

Everyone's heads whipped around to see where it was coming from.

"At last, an adventure that's perfect for me," the voice went on.

"THUNDER!" they all cried. Everyone had forgotten that Thunder could talk on their adventures.

"We've waited six whole adventures for you to say something positive!" Katy teased.

When, finally, they'd each decided that, yes, they were *definitely* still alive, they began to take in the strange, new inky-black world around them. They were in open countryside, standing halfway up a wide, steep hill. At the top, a dark forest loomed ominously, bathed in milky light from the brightest, fullest of moons. Below them, a town was nestled sleepily. It looked more inviting than the forest. Yellow lights shone from the windows of buildings and from street lamps lining the roads and parks. Cars and buses wove in and out, headlights twinkling, making the townscape look and feel magical. The whole town lay under a warm

29

blanket of golden light, its glow seeping into the darkened sky.

"Our town!" Zia cried. "Isn't that the church tower by my house?"

Cassandra nodded. "Yes! And have you noticed the sky over there? You can see what Katy meant about light pollution."

Katy nodded. "I've never seen light pollution so clearly before."

"It's like there's a luminous m-mushroom covering all the buildings," Luca agreed.

"It looks so peaceful from up here," Katy went on.

But even as she said it, a gravelly laugh rumbled up through the ground beneath their feet, followed by a cackle, higher in pitch, but just as menacing.

"What was that?" Zia whispered, clinging to Katy.

30

They froze, listening again, only this time they heard muffled voices.

"Look," said Cassandra, pointing to a small hollow dug into the side of the hill.

"It looks like some kind of lair or burrow," said Thunder, creeping forwards to get a better look. "Yeah, it's definitely home to animals of some kind. Foxes, I bet. Ugh!" He shivered. "I *hate* foxes."

"Don't go too close then," called Katy, reaching through the darkness to pull Thunder back.

But he was already poking his head through the small hole.

"There's a light on down there," he whispered, turning back to his friends. "That's strange."

"A l-light?" asked Luca, looking confused. "Under g-ground?"

"I can hear talking," Thunder continued.

"Can you hear what they're saying?" asked Cassandra.

Thunder took a few tentative steps inside the hollow, pricking up both his ears. He could still hear muffled voices, so, careful not to make a sound, he crawled further in. Moments later, he scrambled back out and joined the others.

"They're definitely foxes," he said, cleaning orange fur and debris from his paws. He sniffed a clump that had snagged on his claws, then pulled a face. "And they're up to something. They mentioned an owl and a feast.

I heard the word 'chaos', then something about turning lights on in the forest. But then it went dark and the voices disappeared. They didn't pass me, so there must be another way out."

Everyone stared back up the hill, expecting the forest to look just as it had before. But another glow had appeared above the trees. Now the forest wasn't only bathed in moonlight from above, but there was a greeny-yellow light, almost fluorescent in appearance, coming from deep within too.

Luca gasped. "I'd expect l-light to be coming from the t-town. N-not the f-forest."

"That *must* be where the foxes went," said Thunder.

"But why would they want to turn lights on in *there*?" asked Katy.

"Good point. Foxes can see in the dark much better than us," said Cassandra. "We need to get to the bottom of this. You heard what Thunder said about the foxes plotting something. Come on. Let's go and find out what they're up to."

CHAPTER FOUR

Zia shot Cassandra a nervous look, her brown eyes wide with fright. "You want *us* to go in *there*?" she asked, pointing up the hill towards the trees.

Cassandra nodded sheepishly. "A playdate adventure wouldn't be the same without a problem to solve, right?" She was trying to make light of her suggestion.

Zia paused for a second, thinking things through. Then: "*Right*," she agreed finally, throwing an arm around Cassandra's shoulder.

"Brilliant!" Luca exclaimed. "Just think of the m-midnight feast waiting for us at the end!" He pointed to the backpack full of treats.

"Exactly!" Cassandra grinned, then hoisted her backpack higher onto her shoulders. "Come on. Last one there is a yucky liquorice allsort!"

As they raced to the top of the hill and neared the edge of the trees, their breathing quickened. They were tired from the climb and Cassandra knew nobody really liked the idea of walking into a deep wood.

"Thunder, could you lead the way from here?" she wheezed, leaning over and resting her hands on top of her knees. Thunder loved being in front and it helped that he could see so well in the dark.

"I thought you'd never ask," he replied, grinning, before disappearing confidently into the trees.

Darkness swallowed them once more. The canopy above was thick with leaves and branches, leaving only tiny gaps for the moonlight to shine through. The wisps of silvery light contrasted with the blackness of the forest, casting stripy shadows across the adventurers as they edged further in. They held hands in a chain, trying their best to stay close to Thunder. Dried leaves crunched beneath their slippers and they wrapped their dressing gowns more securely around them to shut out the biting chill in the air. Every twig that snapped and branch that cracked made them all jump, not just Zia. They could hear shrieks and hoots and snuffles echoing through the trees, but there were no other signs of creatures in the forest. Maybe they were shy and staying away. Or maybe the sounds were just the wind? Whatever was making them, it felt spooky, and they held on to each other's hands more tightly.

As they walked, Cassandra spotted four small orange ovals glinting in the shadows.

"Over there!" she whispered, her heart quickening as she saw them flash again. "Did anyone else see that?"

"They're definitely eyes," said Thunder. "I think the foxes are watching us."

Everyone froze to the spot and peered into the darkness. But no sooner had Thunder spoken, than the eyes disappeared.

"Maybe we should head back," suggested Zia, swallowing hard.

Katy reached through the dark and pulled her in for a hug. "We're scared too," she whispered, squeezing her friend tightly. "But the Playdate Adventure Club *never* gives up. You taught us that, remember? If we stick together, I'm sure we'll be safe."

Zia nodded her head slowly. "OK, I'm all right to go a *little* further. But if we don't find where the light is coming from soon, can we turn around?"

Cassandra nodded. "I think we're close, though. In fact, I'm sure of it. The further we walk, the lighter it seems to be getting."

They edged deeper still, continuing to hold hands in a chain. Cassandra was right – it was dim rather than dark now and they could make out the path in front of them more clearly. They were moving faster, feeling braver. They were just squeezing their way around a labyrinth of thick tree trunks, careful not to trip over the large, snake-like tree roots turning the forest floor into a natural obstacle course, when they saw an eerie glow up ahead. They clambered over more roots and a fallen log, around another gnarled tree trunk, and then:

41

"What *is* that?" Cassandra cried.

"IT'S SO BEAUTIFUL!" Katy gasped.

In the middle of a small clearing, they saw what looked like a giant lantern, glowing a bright, fluorescent greeny-yellow. It was made from an intricate construction of twigs, while the light inside seemed to be pulsing, as though alive.

Zia took a few steps closer, straining to get a better look.

"It's full of insects," she whispered, pointing to the lantern where, inside, they could now make out a collection of hundreds – no, *thousands* – of beetle-like bugs packed tightly together with brightly glowing abdomens.

"They must be glow worms. My mum's told me about them before. Only the females glow. The light is made by a chemical reaction in their bodies – it's called bioluminescence, I think."

Zia's mum was a scientist and Zia always knew lots of exciting facts.

"This has to be the foxes," said Thunder. "I bet this is what they meant when they talked about turning lights on in the forest."

"They must have been c-collecting them for ages," said Luca. "But why are they d-doing this?"

Before anyone could reply, something small crash-landed in front of them. It rolled over and over, feet and wings in a tangle of claws and feathers, and came to a stop just by Zia's slippers.

"Is it alive?" called Thunder.

"Should we touch it?" suggested Katy.

Zia crouched low, but as she stretched out her hand, the creature started to wriggle. With some effort, it got to its tiny feet and shook itself down, puffing out soft tawny feathers and flapping short, stumpy wings. It was a miniature owl, with a tiny beak and enormous round eyes.

"*What time is it? What time is it?*" the owl started squawking, waddling one way, then the other. "*What time is it?*" it cried again, swaying from foot to foot and rotating its head round in the way only owls can do.

"Do you think it's lost?" whispered Katy.

"*What time is it?*" the owl cried once more, before stopping, finally, and peering up at the five strange faces staring down from above.

"Er, hi!" said Cassandra, dropping to her knees so she was closer to the owl's level. "I don't know the *exact* time. But it's evening. Maybe coming up to eleven o'clock?"

The owl staggered again, wide eyes to the ground, and muttered: "*No time, no time!*"

"Um, are you OK?" Katy asked it, kneeling beside Cassandra. "Only, you seem a bit confused."

The owl blinked rapidly, as if trying to block out the glare from the lantern. Then it took a deep breath, composing itself before beginning to speak.

CHAPTER FIVE

"I'm Esra," the little owl said. "It means 'travels at night'. Although now I don't know when to fly because night looks like day and dark is light." The owl's voice sounded more grown-up than they'd expected, wiser than her tiny size would suggest. "And they have to stop before everything's ruined!"

The friends frowned at each other. The owl wasn't making sense.

"Who has to stop?" asked Katy softly.

"The foxes!"

The friends glanced at each other again. Did Esra know what the foxes were up to?

"Perhaps you can start from the beginning," Cassandra encouraged her. She sat cross-legged on the cold forest floor, pulling her dressing gown over her legs to keep warm. The others did the same – even Thunder climbed onto Katy's lap and nestled down, making himself comfortable as they listened to what Esra had to say.

Esra sighed, then puffed out her tiny feathers. "Well…it's complicated, and I don't have much time. You'll need to listen carefully."

Everyone nodded and the little owl took a deep breath.

"Whenever there's a lunar eclipse, like tonight, the night and day animals gather for a feast at midnight. It's a tradition that stretches back to when this forest was young."

Cassandra's heart leapt. Surely they couldn't

be *that* lucky to have chosen an adventure on the night of an actual midnight feast?

"It's our way of marking a truce between the forest creatures – big and small, predator and prey, nocturnal and diurnal," Esra continued.

Katy's hand shot up. It felt like they were in school.

"What's *di-urnal?*" she asked the owl.

Esra sighed. "Diurnal animals are awake during the day. They're the opposite of nocturnal animals, who are awake at night."

"But apart from you, we haven't seen any animals," Katy said.

Esra puffed out her feathers again. "They're probably hiding – they won't be used to seeing humans in the forest."

The friends glanced around, wondering what animals might be hidden among the trees. Esra continued.

"The feasts are important to us. Coming together is our way of showing that *every* animal is crucial to the biodiversity of the forest."

This time, Cassandra's hand shot up. "What's biodiversity?" she asked.

Esra clicked her beak. "It's the huge variety of life – animals *and* plants – that live in the forest. We survive only because we exist together and rely on each other for food."

They nodded again, and Esra took another deep breath.

"At each lunar eclipse – that's when a full moon moves into the Earth's shadow – one animal is tasked with organising the feast. This time, it's me. The invitations have been sent out, but I still need to gather more feast provisions and carry them to the lake at the centre of the forest. The celebration takes place on a small island there. Thanks to those foxes, some animals won't make it, and the feast won't be ready in time for those that do!"

Thunder stretched his front paws out. "Foxes cause trouble where we live too," he tutted, cleaning behind his ears.

Katy stroked Thunder's back then turned to look at Esra. "We think they've been tracking us through the forest."

"They're plotting something," added Zia. "Thunder overheard them in their den – talking about an owl and a feast. It's all starting to make sense now."

Esra nodded and placed her wings over her tiny ears. "It's because they haven't been invited," she said, clicking her beak again. "They caused havoc at the last feast. They'd been warned before, but they didn't listen. They stole food, started a fight and threw our precious feast treats into the lake. The animals held a meeting and decided that this time the foxes wouldn't be welcome. So now they're angry and getting revenge."

"Is that what the l-lights are about?" asked Luca.

"Yes, the lanterns!" Esra flapped her tiny wings up and down. "The foxes have placed four of them around the forest – just like this one here. The lanterns have been glowing every night for a week, so now it's light when it should be dark. We're all mixed up! The foxes aren't affected by them – they can scavenge when it's light *or* dark. But now day animals are awake when they should be sleeping, and night animals are blinded by the light. They can't forage for food or sneak up on their prey. I'm nocturnal, so I see best in the dark – in this light, I keep bumping into trees, hitting my head and feeling dizzy."

"Is that what happened to you just now?" asked Thunder, sounding sorry for the little owl.

"Yes! And now my head has a lump. I'm worn out, and I still haven't gathered enough supplies for the feast. Tonight's celebration is going to be a disaster."

"We can help!" Cassandra interjected. "Can't we?" she asked, turning to her friends.

"You can?" asked Esra.

"Of course," everyone chorused.

Cassandra walked over to the lantern. The fluorescent light coming from the glow worms' abdomens really did look enchanted – like no light she'd seen before. No wonder the animals had mixed-up body clocks.

Thunder joined her. "It's obvious, isn't it?" he said, a know-it-all grin on his face. "We just need to turn off the lights."

Zia followed, bending low and scratching Thunder between his ears. "I'd usually be the last person to say this, but I think you're right."

"And when the l-lights are off," added Luca,

55

joining them, "the animals' b-body clocks should return to n-normal."

"*Then* we can help Esra get ready for the feast!" Katy exclaimed.

CHAPTER SIX

Esra's brow furrowed into a frown.

"I'm afraid it's not that easy," she muttered, hopping over to the lantern while shielding her eyes with her tiny wings. "I've tried opening these lanterns and letting the poor glow worms free. But foxes are cunning. By the time I've moved to the next one, they've rounded up the glow worms and locked them back inside. The light shines brightly again and it's a big waste of my time. The foxes are watching everything we do."

Everyone peered nervously into the trees. Could they see two pairs of bright orange ovals again, glinting at them through the shadows?

"Then maybe we split up," whispered Cassandra. She placed her hand reassuringly on Zia's shoulder. "I know the Playdate Adventure Club always sticks together, but I actually don't think we have the time right now."

"I think you're right," Zia agreed. "Even though I'd obviously prefer us to stick together." She took a deep breath and smiled at her friends.

Cassandra squeezed Zia's shoulder gently, then drew everyone in closer. "If the foxes are watching, surely this is the best place to start. Thunder and Katy, you could hide close by and wait for the foxes. You can stop them gathering up glow worms and convince them to put an end to their tricks. Zia, perhaps you could join forces with Esra and help gather forest treats.

She knows the forest best, so you'll be safe with her. Here's my backpack – there's plenty of space," she said, taking it off her shoulders and handing it to her friend. "Luca, could you stay here with me and help release the glow worms? If Esra's right, as soon as we move on to the next one, the foxes will appear – that's when Thunder and Katy can step in!"

"But how will you find all the lanterns?" Katy asked. "We walked a long way through the forest and this is the first one we've seen."

"I've wondered about that too." Cassandra's shoulders slumped, but Esra was quick to come to the rescue.

"You can always navigate by the moon," she explained. "That's how nocturnal animals travel – by watching the moon and stars. It's difficult now because the lanterns make it trickier to see the night sky. But the moon is directly above the lake. The lanterns have been placed in a circle around it to make it harder to get there. That's why you didn't spot them until you were deep inside the forest. Look," she said, pointing her wing towards the sky, "the moon's already entered the Earth's shadow. That means we don't have much time."

Everyone turned their eyes to where Esra was pointing and saw that the full moon wasn't round anymore. There was a dark smudge covering a part of it – like it was gradually being rubbed out.

"So, if we keep the moon in our vision and walk in a circle around it, we should find all four lanterns?" asked Cassandra.

"Exactly," Esra nodded, and Cassandra gave the little bird a goodbye hug.

It felt strange going their separate ways, but they didn't have a choice if they wanted to save the midnight moon feast. Cassandra and Luca watched as Katy and Thunder disappeared into the shadows to sit and wait for the foxes. Zia offered her arm to Esra (she didn't want the little owl bumping into any more trees), and as soon as Esra hopped on, they hurried off towards the lake to gather forest treats.

The cousins waited for their friends to move further away, then crouched down to inspect the lantern.

"I c-can't see an opening," said Luca, picking it up carefully and turning it slowly around in his hands. He staggered for a moment under its weight and size. Almost dropped it. It was made from a cradle of twigs and branches, tied together at the top and bottom with strips of silvery bark.

Katy was right – the light coming from the

glow worms really was beautiful. Cassandra had to shield her eyes from the glare. She knew foxes were cunning creatures, but she had no idea they could make anything so clever. She squinted her eyes to find the opening.

"How about there?" she said after a while, pointing to a knobbly bit sticking out from one of the twigs. She held on to the knob carefully with her thumb and index finger.

At once, a little door swung open and hundreds of glow worms tumbled to the ground before scuttling away into the forest. They created a fluorescent, serpent-like pathway, slithering silently into the undergrowth, where they eventually disappeared into the shadows.

At once, Cassandra and Luca were plummeted into darkness – like a light switch had been turned off in their part of the forest.

"That w-was easier than I thought," whispered Luca, leaning in close to his cousin's ear. "Do you think the f-foxes are watching?"

"Maybe," Cassandra whispered back. "Let's not stick around to find out. We need to get to the next lantern!"

They looked up at the rubbed-out moon above – and Cassandra gasped.

"Why's it turning orange?" she asked.

Luca creased his forehead in thought. "I think it's to do with the e-eclipse, and Earth being between the moon and the sun. I'm sure I read that the sun's light b-bends around Earth's atmosphere and reflects off the m-moon's surface, making it glow a different colour."

Cassandra hugged her cousin tightly, grateful to have him by her side. Then they took one more look at the milky-orange moon above their heads and hurried off in search of lantern number two.

Meanwhile, Katy was hunched low, concealed within a thick bush of thorny branches. Thunder waited patiently between her slippers, peering out through the wings of her dressing gown.

Cassandra and Luca had barely left the clearing when two devious-looking foxes emerged from the shadows.

"I knew it!" Thunder shuddered.

Katy pulled her cat into her arms.

"I know you don't like foxes. But we're not here to pick a fight. We need to show the foxes what happens when they play havoc with the ecosystem. Esra's counting on us."

65

Thunder raised his paw in a salute. "Aye aye, Captain!"

Katy grinned. "OK," she said, watching the foxes root around for the glow worms. "I'd better take that lantern apart so they can't refill it. I need you to distract them somehow. At least one light will be out of action then, even if those pesky foxes won't listen to what we have to say."

CHAPTER SEVEN

Katy stayed low and crept towards the lantern while Thunder moved stealthily towards the foxes. The two creatures looked up just as he emerged from the shadows. There was an evil glint in their eyes – mischievous, cunning, eager to cause trouble. But Thunder was ready for them. He knew exactly what he had to do.

"What have we here?" asked the bigger of the two foxes. This one had a thick scar running along its snout.

"We *like* cats, don't we, Ned?" said the other sarcastically. This fox was smaller, with a bushier, white-tipped tail and a rustier-coloured coat.

"To eat, you mean?" mocked Ned, snapping his jaws at Thunder. "Oh yes, a cat will be quite the treat at our own midnight feast tonight."

Thunder stalked back and forth, head high, trying to give the impression of a cat that's not easily intimidated. "But how does it feel not to be invited to the *real* midnight feast?" he asked. "You were so badly behaved at the last one, no one wants you at tonight's celebration. It can't feel nice to be excluded."

The foxes frowned at each other before bursting into fits of laughter.

"You think we care what others think?"

asked Ned. He scratched at his neck – Thunder hoped he didn't have fleas. "Did you hear that, Nina? This cat thinks we *mind* being banned from the feast."

Nina – the smaller fox – broke into a high-pitched cackle. "That is funny!" she cried. "Who wants to go to Esra's silly midnight moon feast anyway."

"We'll have our own celebration – and now we have the *purr*-fect dish to serve," mocked Ned.

Nina clutched at her tummy and chortled loudly. "*Purr*-fect dish," she repeated. "That's a good one, Ned."

Thunder scowled as the two foxes continued laughing at Ned's joke.

"What's wrong? Are you not *feline* well?" Ned guffawed.

"Would you like us to *paws* this conversation?" Nina howled.

69

Katy tutted to herself as she listened to the foxes. Poor Thunder, having to put up with such terrible cat jokes. At least his distraction tactics were working.

The foxes had their backs to Katy, who was only inches away from the lantern now. Her fingers stretched out to reach it – just one more step…

Nina's head flicked round and she leapt swiftly on top of the lantern, pinning it between her front two paws.

"Well, well, well, another stray," Nina snapped, smiling maliciously at Katy.

"Trying to steal our lantern, are we?" asked Ned.

By now, he'd lost interest in Thunder and was closing in on Katy, licking his lips and baring his teeth. "Now our feast is going to be even better than we'd hoped."

Katy had had enough. Who did the foxes think they were?

"You think you'll be eating us?" she asked boldly, getting to her feet, hands on hips. "If you do, you know you'll *never* be invited to join a moon feast again."

The foxes laughed.

"But we don't care," barked Ned.

"You've said that already," Katy replied, sounding very teacher like. "The thing is, *I* don't believe you."

"And neither do I," Thunder followed. "I'm sure you'll care *deeply* when there's no food left to eat because the food chain has broken down!"

"If that happens, some animals will be left with nothing to eat, and that will change the forest forever!" Katy added. "Animals thrive best when they exist together. It's why your feast is important – because it celebrates *all* life in the forest – and why ecosystems shouldn't be tampered with."

"I hadn't thought of that," mumbled Nina.

"Neither had I," said Ned, pawing the ground.

"So, what do you suggest?" asked Nina. She was sitting on her hind legs now, scratching her head with her front paw.

"An apology," said Katy. "You weren't invited today because you weren't sorry about the way you behaved at the last feast. And you're still causing chaos."

"If you keep lighting up the forest at night, things will only get worse," explained Thunder.

"Eventually, there could be no more animals left to hunt," warned Katy.

"Which means no more food for you to eat," said Thunder. "Ever!"

The foxes exchanged a nervous look.

"Only saying sorry and changing your ways will set things right," Katy went on.

"But you have to mean it if you really want the forest to thrive," Thunder said.

Katy glanced at Thunder. Had they done it? Had they convinced the foxes to change their ways?

Nina put the lantern down and turned to look at Ned.

"I do love our home," she said. "*And* a midnight moon feast. The food is delicious."

"But it's too late, remember?" Ned sighed.

"The feast isn't ready!"

"Of course!" Nina kicked her legs out and slumped heavily to the floor. "The forest creatures are all tired."

"No one's in the mood," moaned Ned.

Katy looked at Thunder, nervous energy bubbling up inside her.

"It's *never* too late." Thunder grinned. "If you're ready to say sorry, you just need to follow us."

CHAPTER EIGHT

Zia spotted a plump mushroom sticking out between the roots of an oak tree. She bent down and tugged it from the earth, feeling excitement building as she stuffed it into her bag. Earlier, when Esra had talked about gathering treats for the midnight moon feast, Zia thought the little owl had meant a few acorns, maybe, or just a small handful of berries. But they were collecting anything and everything they could find in the forest – leaves, stones, sticks, nuts, flowers, pine needles, pinecones.

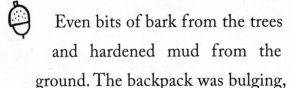

Even bits of bark from the trees and hardened mud from the ground. The backpack was bulging, and Zia didn't think she could carry much more.

"Do forest animals really eat all *this*?" Zia asked, heaving the bag onto her back.

"Oh yes," Esra replied, still perched on Zia's shoulder. "Every part of the forest sustains us."

"Even mud?" asked Zia, frowning.

Esra flew to the ground and began scratching at the hard earth with her claws. She uncovered what looked like an old acorn, a tiny green root sprouting from one end. "Look." She grinned. "It's what's *inside* that has the potential to surprise us."

Zia thought for a second. "Maybe that's why I'm not feeling so frightened anymore. Because now I've met you, I know it isn't just scary things that live in the dark."

Esra stopped foraging and peered wisely up at Zia. "Your world is light, mine is dark. It's easy to be scared of things that aren't familiar. But when you get used to something different, those fears often begin to slip away."

Zia looked all around her then, a warm feeling spreading across her tummy. The night was getting darker – she wondered if this was because of the eclipse, or if the lanterns were finally going out – but with Esra beside her, she didn't feel so afraid.

She gazed up towards the moon and sighed contentedly. It was turning orange, like someone had coloured it in with a giant felt-tip pen.

"You know there are eight phases of the moon?" Esra explained. "And each impacts our world in different ways. They affect the tides in the seas and light in the night sky, even how plants and creatures behave."

"That's incredible," Zia replied, bringing her eyes back to face the little owl. "I've seen a full moon before – like tonight – and a crescent moon, but I didn't realise there were others."

Esra picked up a twig and started making marks in the hardened earth.

"The phases always go in order. There's the new moon – it looks like this," she said, drawing a circle and shading it in. "Then there's the waxing crescent –" this moon drawing looked like a banana "– the first quarter, waxing gibbous, full moon –" Esra now drew a large circle "– waning gibbous, last quarter and, finally, the waning crescent. After that, it goes back to the beginning and the sequence starts all over again."

"But why *does* the moon change shape?" Zia asked when Esra had finished. "I mean, why isn't it always round? Or in a crescent?"

Esra pointed back up to the sky. The moon was almost directly over their heads now, which meant they must be very close to the lake in the middle of the forest.

"The moon doesn't really change shape," Esra explained, flying back onto Zia's shoulder.

"We just see the parts of it lit up by the sun. As the moon goes round the Earth, different portions of it reflect the sun's light, making it seem as if it's changing shape. Actually, it's our view of the moon that's changing."

Zia nodded, fascinated by everything Esra was telling her.

"But we need to move quickly now," the owl continued. "Have you noticed the moon turning a darker orange? That means the lunar eclipse has started. It's almost midnight."

They navigated their way around a cluster of tree trunks until they were standing on the shores of a wide, circular lake. The water was still as glass, the moon reflecting perfectly on its surface.

"I knew it," Esra cried. "Animals are arriving already!" She moved her wing in an arc and Zia saw a herd of deer on the far bank, a swan gliding past, a grey squirrel scampering along a log towards the water.

Then she noticed two other figures – these ones more human in form. They were waving their arms and jumping up and down.

"Cassie! Luca!" Zia squealed and ran towards her friends. "I've missed you so much. Were you able to find the lanterns and free the glow worms?"

"Yes!" said Cassandra, beaming.

"The h-hardest part was finding the lanterns, but Esra's instructions helped a lot." Luca smiled at Esra, who was still perched on Zia's shoulder. "We kept the m-moon in our sight at all times."

Esra flapped her tiny wings. "I can't believe it!" she hooted. "There are no more lights in our forest and we have enough treats for the feast. Thank you. *Thank you!* But now we have to move quickly. It's almost time for the full eclipse. Everyone, follow me."

She took off into the air and glided gracefully across the water. In the middle, rising up above its glassy surface, was an island that looked like the hump of a whale. It was smooth, dark and round in shape.

Zia frowned. None of them could fly, so how would they get to the island? She didn't fancy getting wet.

They stood in a line, watching as Esra came in to land, and that's when they noticed a zigzag of stones poking up from the surface of the water. Two, three, four – as many as twenty or thirty stones forming a walkway from the place they were standing to where Esra had started setting up for the feast. Animals were already hurrying across them, eager to get to the celebration on time.

"Stepping stones!" cried Zia excitedly. "Come on. Esra's waiting!"

"But how about Katy and Thunder?" Cassandra asked. "Should we wait for them?"

"I c-could stay here?" suggested Luca. "You two can h-help Esra set up for the feast."

Cassandra gave her cousin a high five. "You know, our club has become even better with you in it." Then she turned to Zia. "Do you want me to carry the backpack? It looks really heavy – you've obviously been busy."

Zia nodded gratefully and Cassandra unhooked the bag from her friend's shoulders. Then, holding their arms out for balance, they tiptoed carefully across the stones.

CHAPTER NINE

Luckily, the stepping stones were wider and closer together than they'd appeared from the bank. The moisture on their surface glistened like precious jewels in the moonlight. It felt like a magical walkway to an enchanted world.

As Zia and Cassandra neared the island, they were held up behind an elderly badger. The badger was tired now and too weak to walk any further.

"Let me help," said Cassandra kindly, bending down and lifting the animal into her arms.

Within moments, she'd safely deposited it onto dry land. Zia arrived soon after, followed by two moles, a family of rabbits, three field mice and a hedgehog. The animals kept on coming, some paddling on logs across the water.

Cassandra and Zia looked around. There were no trees on the island, just thick grass to sit on, surrounded by inky-blue water. The wide night sky stretched above them, gently lit by a faint glow of orange from the eclipse of the moon. They couldn't think of a more perfect place to enjoy their midnight feast.

Cassandra set the rucksack down and everyone helped unload the feast provisions. The grass was soft as a blanket, and Zia was just adding Thunder's biscuits to the impressive-looking collection of treats when they heard voices from across the water. They turned to see a large fluffy cat leaping nimbly across the stones, followed by Katy and Luca, shouting and waving their arms.

"You made it!" Cassandra and Zia cried in unison. It felt like a lifetime since they'd all been together. They charged over and gathered their friends in the biggest group hug.

"Did you meet the foxes?" asked Zia when the hug fell apart.

"Are they going to let us have our feast in peace?" asked Cassandra.

But it was impossible to hear their answers because a rumble echoed all around them, gradually getting louder, like an orchestra's crescendo. Through the darkness, across lake and sky, throngs of forest creatures were hurrying towards them. There were herds of deer clattering across the stones, bats and birds of prey swooping down from the sky. There were robins and sparrows and other birds they recognised from their gardens. Squirrels and field mice and badgers and voles.

In the water, they could now make out ducks, geese and swans, otters and weasels. Every forest creature – nocturnal and diurnal, big and small – that had received an invitation to tonight's midnight moon feast. Creatures who, until Cassandra and Luca had turned off the lanterns, had felt as tired and mixed up as Esra had been.

Esra pointed to the moon, which had almost completely moved into the Earth's shadow. She flew on to Zia's shoulder. "Welcome!" she called, when the final animal – a regal-looking stag – was settled among them and the clamour had quietened down. "It's almost midnight, yet I didn't think tonight's feast would happen. Some of you have been awake when you should have been sleeping. Some have been hungry when you should have been hunting. And all because of two mischievous foxes."

A gravelly voice cut through the dark: "We're sorry."

Everyone gasped as Ned and Nina pushed themselves cagily to the front of the crowd.

"We promise we'll be good from now on." Nina coughed.

"We didn't mean to cause trouble," mumbled Ned, looking embarrassed.

Esra hopped along the ground until she was only inches from the foxes' noses. She placed her wings on feathery hips and angled her head up to look into their scheming eyes. "But why should we believe you?"

"Because..." Ned sighed, mustering up the courage. "Because every animal deserves another chance. I promise, we've changed our ways."

Katy nodded. "It's true," she said, smiling at the others. "We've spent a long time talking about it. A leopard may not be able to change its spots, but these foxes can. Ned and Nina won't be giving you any more trouble."

Esra was silent for a moment, hopping in circles around the two wily creatures while she considered their apology. The other forest animals started to stir, stamping hooves and paws, hooting and braying in anger.

Eventually, Esra held up her wing, calling for silence.

"Our new friends tell me the foxes have changed their ways," she said firmly.

The animals quietened down, curious to hear what Esra and the foxes had to say. The foxes bowed their heads.

"We really are sorry," grovelled Ned again.

"For the chaos we caused last year, and for bringing light into the forest at night," Nina added.

Esra raised a wing once more. "This forest has always been our sanctuary. Away from the light and hazards of the city. You mixed up the natural order of our home."

"We'll never do it again," said Nina.

"Can you forgive us?" asked Ned.

Esra looked back at the crowd of animals who were waiting to take their lead from the little owl. Their expressions had started to soften.

"I'd like a show of paws, hooves, feet or wings," she instructed, "from anyone who thinks Ned and Nina deserve another chance."

There was a pause before the first paw stretched timidly into the air. It belonged to a small brown rabbit with floppy ears and a cotton-wool tail. Soon after, the elderly badger raised its paw. More followed, until every creature – including Cassandra and her friends – agreed that the foxes should be forgiven.

Esra smiled. This year, the animals would be feasting together in peace. "Come, it's time for *all* of you to feast."

At once, stars exploded like fireworks in the night sky above them. The lunar eclipse had turned the moon into a brilliant orange orb, burning brightly amid the black, and everyone "oohed" and "aahed" as an orange ray shot down from the sky, bathing the midnight treats in its laser-like spotlight. Slowly, the forest treats started to shimmer – berries, nuts, mushrooms, bits of bark. They all began to morph and change shape, until the midnight moon feast – the one they'd waited all this time for – appeared in front of them: chocolates, doughnuts, ice cream, popcorn, sweets, biscuits in different shapes and sizes, twinkling and sparkling like the brightest of diamonds.

With shouts and cheers of delight, everyone dived in. Ned and Nina were grinning wildly, ecstatic to be part of the celebration. Esra was clutching a shimmering cupcake tightly in her claws, demolishing it with her tiny beak. The elderly badger was stuffing large mouthfuls of rainbow-coloured popcorn into its mouth.

"Didn't I promise the best midnight feast?" Cassandra called to the others as she bit into a moon-shaped biscuit. It crackled in her mouth like popping candy. "Magical treats under a moonlit sky." She beamed at her friends. "You can't get more perfect than this!"

"Esra was right about the forest being full of surprises," said Zia, smiling as she shovelled a heaped spoon of ice cream into her mouth. She'd never tasted a flavour quite like it.

"This feast is incredible, C-Cassie!" Luca exclaimed, lips sticky with candyfloss. "I c-can't believe those f-forest treats turned into *this*!"

"It sure beats eating mice," Thunder said casually, hiccupping as he bit into a bonbon that bubbled in his mouth.

Katy giggled, grabbing a handful of fizzy sweets. "And it definitely makes up for the midnight feast that we slept through."

As they ate, savouring flavours they'd likely never taste again, Esra hopped over to join them. She opened her beak and placed a tiny fleck of light into each of their hands and paws. "Pieces of moonbeam." She smiled. "They're gifts to say thank you. We wouldn't be here if you hadn't helped save the midnight moon feast."

The friends gasped. "Thank you!" they sang out, stunned to have received such an extraordinary gift.

"We promise not to forget you," said Zia, stroking the little owl on her head. "You know, it's thanks to you that I'm not scared of the dark anymore."

"And you've helped us understand the harm that bright lights cause to animals," said Cassandra, smiling warmly.

"We should protect our ecosystems," agreed

Thunder, biting into a doughnut. "Not mess with nature's way of doing things." Silvery jam oozed from its middle, and he licked the stickiness off his paws.

When they'd finished devouring every magical morsel in front of them, they took it in turns to give Esra a goodbye hug.

Katy yawned. "I feel so tired suddenly."

"And m-me," Luca said, catching Katy's yawn and rubbing his eyes. "Even though I d-don't want tonight to end."

"I'm ready for my bed, too," said Cassandra drowsily. She gathered everyone into a circle, pulling a reluctant Thunder into the middle, and they held on to each other's hands. Then they closed their eyes tightly and imagined Cassandra's bedroom back home.

"Repeat after me," Cassandra whispered, "I wish to go home."

"*I wish to go home,*" her friends chanted back.

Immediately, jolts of electricity shot around their bodies. They felt weightless, like they were flying through the sky, floating past an orange moon and shooting around the stars in the sky above. It was only when their bodies felt normal that they dared to open their eyes.

They were back in their own pyjamas in Cassandra's bedroom – camping mats messy on the floor, Luca's telescope its original size on her desk. The curtains were drawn but the light was still on.

"Can somebody turn that off?" asked Zia, grinning while dramatically shielding her eyes from the glare.

"You're sure?" asked Cassandra. She felt proud of her friend. It wasn't easy facing your fears.

Zia nodded and yawned. "I'm so tired as well."

Katy stretched her arms in the air and gazed longingly at her pillow. Thunder was already curled up next to it, paws over his head, fast asleep.

"Bagsy first in bed!" shouted Zia, diving to the floor and climbing into her sleeping bag.

But as Cassandra also snuggled down in bed and pulled her duvet up to her chin, she noticed something new and shiny on the bracelet she always wore on her wrist. It was another charm for their collection – a tiny silver moon, giving off the faintest orangey glow.

"Look!" she whispered. "A new charm!"

Her friends were also wearing a moon charm. Even Thunder had one dangling from his collar, although he didn't know about it yet.

"That was the BEST midnight feast, Cassie."

Katy yawned again, snuggling into her pillow.

"The best midnight *moon* feast," added Zia.

"And the very b-best sleepover ever," said Luca, pulling his sleeping bag over his chin. "But now I n-need to sleep."

"Goodnight." Cassandra yawned, then flicked the switch by her bed.

At once, the room went dark.

How to Reduce Light Pollution

1. Always switch lights off as you leave a room.
2. Avoid lighting up trees where bats and other nocturnal wildlife might live or feed.
3. Use motion sensors or timers so outdoor lights are only on when they need to be.

☆ ☆ ☆ ☆ ☆ ☆

THE DARK

In open countryside on a clear night, you can usually see an incredible two and a half thousand stars in the sky! But in a busy city, because of light polution, you might count fewer than twelve.

Many people are scared of the dark, yet some night-time noises are less scary if you know what they are. The "too-wit too-woo" of an owl, for example, is made by a male and female calling to each other: one saying "too-wit" and the other replying "too-woo"!

Not all nocturnal animals can see brilliantly in the dark. Bats navigate using echolocation, meaning they make sounds that bounce off objects like an echo.

Emma Beswetherick is the mother of two young children and wanted to write exciting, inspirational and enabling adventure stories to share with them. Emma works in publishing and lives in London.

Find her at: emmabeswetherick.com

Anna Woodbine is an independent book designer and illustrator based in the hills near Bath.

Find her at: thewoodbineworkshop.co.uk